D0801513

GREAT ILLUSTRATED CLASSICS

THE SWISS FAMILY ROBINSON

Johann Wyss

adapted by
Eliza Gatewood Warren

Illustrations by
Pablo Marcos Studio

**BARONET
BOOKS**

BARONET BOOKS, New York, New York

SPMIC90758

Contents

About the Author

Johann Rudolf Wyss was born in Bern, Switzerland on March 13, 1781. He was the son of a pastor who entertained young Johann and his brothers at bedtime with adventure tales of a shipwrecked preacher and his family.

Johann had a fine education at several German universities, and in 1806 he became a professor at the University of Bern and also its head librarian. But Professor Wyss never lost his love of literature. This led to his collecting and editing Swiss folk stories and to his writing of the Swiss national anthem.

But it wasn't until 1813 that Johann Wyss gained worldwide fame when he wrote, edited and published his father's bedtime stories under the title of *The Shipwrecked Preacher and His Family: An Instructional Book for Children and Their Friends in City or Country*. This was later to be shortened to the now-famous *Swiss Family Robinson*.

Immediately after its publication, *The Swiss Family Robinson* was translated into many languages, including English. Over the years, it has become one of the most popular books for generations of European and American children—a popularity which Wyss lived to see and enjoy until his death in 1830.

A Violent Storm

CHAPTER 1

Shipwrecked!

Many years ago my family left Switzerland and boarded a ship bound for the sparkling blue waters of the Pacific Ocean. Our destination was an island near New Guinea, where we were to establish a colony. Along the way we ran into a violent storm.

For six days, the wind howled and tore at the sails, while the waves pounded against our little wooden ship, tossing it high in the air.

On the seventh day, the masts ripped apart and fell into the sea. Several leaks appeared, and the ship began to fill with water. Realizing that the storm had driven us far off course, the

7

frightened sailors fell to their knees in prayer.

"You musn't be afraid," I said to my four sons, Fritz, 15, Jack, 13, Ernest, 11, and Francis, 8, who clung to me trembling. "God will save us, for nothing is impossible to him." My wife, Elizabeth, wiped away her tears and reassured our sons that we would survive this crisis. I admired her courage, but my heart was heavy as I led my family in prayer.

"Land ahoy! Land ahoy!" cried a sailor.

At that same moment, the ship crashed into a large rock, sending everyone on board reeling in all directions. Then we heard a loud crack as if the whole ship was falling apart. Suddenly, the sea came rushing in.

"All is lost!" shouted the captain in his booming voice. "Into the boats, men!"

As the terrified sailors rushed by us, Elizabeth and the children looked at me in wide-eyed amazement.

"Stay calm," I said. "There is no reason to panic. First of all, the water hasn't reached us

The Sea Comes Rushing In.

yet, and secondly, we are near land. Wait here in the hold while I go see what is the best thing to do."

On deck, one wave after another knocked me down. When I finally struggled to my feet, I was greeted by a scene of utter disaster. The ship was completely shattered, and there was a large, gaping hole in one side where the water was rushing in. The crew had just cut loose the ropes of the boats and were pushing off into the churning sea.

"Come back!" I shouted, but the angry ocean drowned out my cries.

Soon the boats disappeared from sight. My only consolation was that since the ship's stern was lodged between two rocks, we were safe for the time being. Peering through the rain, I could make out the dim outline of land in the distance.

"With luck and the change of tide, we should be able to reach shore sometime tomorrow," I told my solemn sons when I went below.

"Come Back!"

"Come. Let's eat some dinner," Elizabeth added bravely, sensing my anxiety. "We have a long night ahead of us."

Fritz, my eldest son, who realized the danger we were in, sat up with us long after his brothers fell asleep. "I've been thinking," he said. "If only we had some life jackets, we could swim to shore."

"Good idea, Fritz!" I answered. "Let's see what we can find to make them with."

In the kitchen we uncovered some small wooden butter tubs. We tied these together, two by two, using towels. When we were finished, we had made six life jackets. Delighted with his accomplishment, Fritz curled up near his brothers and fell into a sound sleep. Elizabeth and I, fearing that each strange sound might spell disaster, kept a prayerful watch throughout the long night.

The first rays of morning light awakened the boys, and they rushed up on deck to see a bright sun shining over the Pacific. As we saw

Making Life Jackets from Butter Tubs

that the sea was calm at last, our spirits began to soar.

"Let's put on our new life jackets and swim to shore," Fritz cried.

"Maybe you can swim, Fritz," Jack answered cautiously, still shaken by the desertion of the crew, "but the rest of us can't. We'd soon be drowned. Wouldn't it be better to make a float of rafts and get to land that way?"

"Good thinking, Jack," I said, slapping him on the back. "Get busy, everyone. See what you can find."

When Jack opened the doors of the captain's quarters, his two huge dogs, Turk and Flora, came leaping out. They licked Jack's face and hands hungrily. Jack jumped upon the back of one and, holding tightly to his ears, rode him up on deck.

"Better be careful," I warned. "A hungry dog can be dangerous."

"You'll be glad enough to have these dogs

Jack Finds Turk and Flora.

when we get to land," Jack replied. "They'll be great help hunting and shooting."

"Look what I found!" called a voice from below. Rushing down, we saw four empty casks floating about in the water. We immediately fished them out and sawed them in half, making eight tubs, each big enough to hold one person.

I then salvaged several long planks from the hold and placed the eight tubs upon one, nailing each tub securely to the plank. Then the boys and I nailed two planks on each side of the tubs, creating a narrow but sturdy boat.

After cutting other planks into paddles, we lowered the boat in the water. We were ready to set sail!

"Wait!" cried my wife, scurrying up from another section of the hold. "You won't believe what I've discovered! A cow, a mule, two goats, six sheep, and a pig!" She caught her breath, then went on. "Plus hens, roosters, pigeons. geese, and ducks!

Sawing the Casks

"What a wonderful find!" I exclaimed. "But we can take only the roosters and hens with us this trip."

I then tucked them in the tub that already held the gunpowder, threw the pigeons up in the air, and put the other fowl in the water. The provisions filled another tub, leaving each member of the family with his own individual tub to ride in.

"I shall never muster enough courage to get into one of these," said Elizabeth nervously.

"Come now, dear wife, I think your tub is a better sailing ship than the wreck we're leaving behind." I took her by the arm and gently guided her into the little round vessel.

"We're off!" I yelled as we pushed away from our wrecked ship. Turk and Flora swam after us, along with all the cackling geese and ducks. The sea was calm, and the sky was bright blue with not a cloud in sight. Paddling along, we passed chests and casks from the shipwreck, and managed to seize two of them

18

"We're Off!"

and pull them aboard.

As we approached land, we saw that the coastline was rocky and barren on one side and green and lush on the other. Suddenly, we hit a swift current, which swept us toward the rocky coast and into a little opening between the rocks. That opening was the mouth of a small creek.

Standing on the banks of the creek as it widened into a river, calmly watching our arrival was a family of penguins, while pink flamingoes soared over our heads, flapping their wings to wish us a warm welcome.

"We're safe!" cried the boys, jumping out as we touched land. Elizabeth and I gathered our family around us and thanked God for a peaceful landing. Our hearts were full of joy.

After unloading the boat, we pitched a tent near a brook and made beds of dried grass. Elizabeth helped us construct a crude kitchen, and she began preparations for dinner.

While I was dragging the two casks up from

A Warm Welcome from the Penguins

the shore, the boys set out explore the area. Jack found a giant lobster, and Ernest discovered an oyster bed. Fritz, returning from the other side of the creek, brought back an agouti, a native pig. He told of beautiful woods and fields, with soft, green grass for our animals to eat.

"Tomorrow, we'll return to the wreck and bring all the animals here," I assured him. "Did you see any trace of the crew?"

But neither Fritz nor the others had seen even a glimpse of the sailors.

After dinner as the sun sank in the west, we retired to our tent. We had been through a frightful ordeal, but we were grateful to be alive and to be together. And so it was that my family, shipwrecked at sea, spent their first night on a desert island somewhere in the South Pacific.

The First Night on a Desert Island

Making Plans for the Day

CHAPTER 2

Return to the Wreck

The next day, we were awakened at dawn by the crowing of the roosters just outside our tent. Over a breakfast of lobster meat and biscuits, Elizabeth and I made plans for our first full day on the island.

"Don't you think you should investigate the land on the other side of the river and see if it's as lush and green as Fritz says it is?" she asked.

"You're right," I told her. "We definitely should compare the two areas before deciding where to build our home."

"Keep your eyes open for any sign of the

crew," Elizabeth called as Fritz and I started on our journey

With this in mind, we chose a path near the shore so that we would be in a position to spot the sailors quickly. But alas! There was no one in sight. All we could see was the wreck bobbing up and down in the azure-blue sea.

We had just crossed a shallow part of the river when Turk came bounding up and, taking the lead, guided us through the tall grass and tangled vegetation to the top of a hill.

The world we discovered that day was truly a tropical paradise. We passed through forests of towering trees of all types, fields of sugar cane, and rolling hills of grass, leafy green plants, and fragrant flowers. Brightly-colored birds darted across our path, and monkeys chatted in the trees as they watched our every move.

At noontime, we entered a forest of palm trees. The monkeys, frightened by Turk's

No One in Sight

barking, scurried to the tree-tops. From there, they watched as we ate our lunch of leftover lobster and biscuits, making hostile noises and grinding their teeth all the while.

Suddenly, Fritz leaped to his feet. "Father, I have an idea," he cried. "I'm going to put these monkeys to work!"

With that, he began throwing stones at the tree-tops. This infuriated the monkeys, and they began tearing off all the coconuts they could reach and hurling them down at us.

Laughing loudly at the success of his scheme, Fritz opened up some of the coconuts with his hatchet. He passed one to me, and we thirstily drank the milk, which we both agreed was not all that tasty.

In late afternoon we headed for home, weighted down by a sack of Fritz's coconuts, a large bundle of sugar cane, and a collection of plates, bowls, and spoons that we had fashioned from gourds.

Along the way we had still another tussle

Coconuts Come Hurling Down.

with a troop of monkeys, this time on the ground. Turk, barking loudly, charged into their midst and brutally attacked a female monkey who was cradling a baby in her arms.

"No, Turk!" Fritz shouted, rushing to the rescue.

But it was too late. Turk not only killed the monkey, but he completely devoured her as well. At first, her little orphaned baby hid in the grass. but then he scampered out and climbed up on Fritz's shoulders.

"Father, Father, can't I take him home with me?" Fritz begged. "I will feed him my share of the coconut milk and take good care of him."

"All right. Bring him along," I replied. "I suppose it's the least we can do."

"No bigger than a kitten, the little monkey rode gleefully home on Fritz's shoulders. They were greeted with shouts of welcome by the other boys, and the monkey soon became a real family favorite.

"Can't I Take Him Home with Me?"

Elizabeth was delighted with our haul, and she showed us how she, too, had been busy while we were gone. She had made a turnspit on which little Francis was now roasting a goose. Beneath the goose, she had spread out oyster shells to make a perfect drip pan.

"You know, my dear," I said after I had taken my first bite of the goose, "I do think the land we explored today would make us a good home. However, before I begin such a project, I think we should bring the animals in from the wreck."

"I'm sure you're right," Elizabeth said, passing around some Dutch cheese from one of the casks. "Otherwise they will wash away in the first rough sea."

"Fritz and I will leave at dawn. I don't like leaving you and the other boys alone, so before we go, I will erect a pole with a white sail flying. If an emergency arises, take down the sail and fire a gun three times."

With the signal pole erected, Fritz and I

Roast Goose and Cheese for Dinner

sailed back to the wreck early in the morning. The first thing we did was to load up six of the tubs with the provisions we found on board: kitchen utensils, a silver service, metal plates, chests of wine and butter, hams, sausages, sacks of grain and potatoes, farm implements, hammocks, and blankets. Filled to the brim now, the tubs sat dangerously low in the water.

Fritz then attached a sail and a rudder to our little ship to help speed the voyage back to land.

"Perhaps we could make a raft for all the animals," he suggested.

"Now, son, how could we persuade a cow, a mule, six sheep, two goats, and a pig to get on a raft, much less remain still long enough to ride to shore? No, we'll have to think of something else."

"How about life jackets?" Fritz cried. "We can make each animal a life jacket!"

At first I laughed, but then I decided it was

34

Fritz Attaches a Sail to the Little Ship.

worth a try. Each life jacket consisted of two casks, one on either side of the animal. These were tied together by leather thongs, with a large cork underneath for buoyancy. One by one, each animal was fitted with his life jacket, then pushed into the sea. After only a moment under water, the animals quickly bobbed upand began swimming toward the shore.

Mighty proud of ourselves and in high spirits over the success of our experiment, Fritz and I hopped in the two empty tubs, one on each end of the boat.

"We're off!" I shouted.

With the wind filling our new sail, it took no time to get halfway to land.

Suddenly, Fritz grabbed me by the arm. "Father, Father, look what's coming!"

I turned my head just in time to see a big slippery creature rise to the surface, then plunge beneath the waves again. I sat frozen, for heading straight toward the animals was the biggest shark I had ever seen!

The Animals Swim Toward the Shore.

Fritz Fires Two Shots at the Shark.

CHAPTER 3

The Nonsuch Bridge

"Fritz, get your gun ready!" I cried. "Fire the moment the shark is close enough! "

Moving with the speed of lightning, the fish headed for the boat. Reaching the animals first, it attacked one of the sheep. Fritz fired two shots, which hit the shark in the head. Wounded, the creature turned in the water and hurried off to sea, leaving behind a long, bloody trail.

Breathing a sigh of relief, we quickly guided our craft into shore. As we landed, Elizabeth and the boys came running up to welcome us home. Laughing loudly at the sight of the animals in life jackets, the boys helped remove them. One by one, the animals went lumbering down the sandy shore to explore their new island home.

"I have something for you, my dear," I said, handing Elizabeth the ham from one of the tubs. "This will feed us for some time to come."

"And I have found something in the sand that will make a delicious side dish," she answered, smiling. With that, she produced a dozen turtle eggs she had been hiding behind her back.

"See, Father," said Ernest, "they're just like the ones Robinson Crusoe found on *his* island."

"What a wonderful supper we shall have!" cried Francis, clapping his hands.

That night, Elizabeth spread a tablecloth on the end of the butter cask and set the table with the plates and spoons from the ship. She placed the ham in the middle, with cheeses

Removing the Animals' Life Jackets

and a turtle omelet on either side.

By and by, all the animals came and assembled around us as we ate this tasty meal. We felt like the kings of a grand new country!

As we were finishing this feast, Elizabeth burst out, "I cannot wait to tell you my news. While you were gone, I decided to see for myself what the land on the other side of the creek was like, and I found the most beautiful woods you can ever imagine! Actually, it is a grove of fourteen of the tallest and broadest trees in the world. And each tree is supported on either side by giant arches, formed from the roots. I do believe it's the perfect spot for our new home!"

"But, my dear, we are fine right here," I protested. "We are near the ship, which still has some valuable supplies on board. And we are protected on all sides by these rocks."

"But wild animals could leap over those rocks in a minute," Elizabeth argued gently. "And I have everything I want from the ship.

Kings of a Grand New Country!

Besides, it frightens me to have you sailing that treacherous sea."

"We shall have to give the matter careful consideration," I said. "If we are to leave this place, we will have to build a bridge across the river.

"But that will take such a long time!" Elizabeth cried.

Despite Elizabeth's concern, the construction of the bridge—the Nonsuch Bridge, as we called it—took place in only one day. Luckily we found all the timber and planks we needed on a nearby islet and carried them back to our island on the boat. Then we harnassed the cow and the mule with ropes, so they could pull the lumber to the site of the bridge.

With the lumber there, I had to devise a plan for laying the timbers across the eighteen-foot expanse of river. After much deliberation, I decided first to attach one end of a plank to the trunk of a tree by a long cord. I then fastened a second long cord to the other end of the plank.

The Cow and Mule Pull the Lumber.

THE SWISS FAMILY ROBINSON

To the free end of the cord I tied a rock, which I then tossed across to the opposite bank.

I immediately crossed the river and fastened a pulley onto a tree there. Untying the rock, I then passed the loose end of the cord through the pulley. With this cord in my hand, I recrossed the river. Next, I attached the cord to the mule and the cow, who slowly but surely began to move. Braying and mooing all the while, they gradually pulled the plank across the river. To my great joy, I saw it touch the other side and become permanently fixed there.

"We did it! We did it! We built the bridge!" yelled Fritz as he and Jack bounded quickly over it.

We laid a second and a third plank the same way, and soon we had a broad and handsome bridge over which to safely travel.

Once the bridge was completed, we loaded all our provisions on the cow and the mule. With each of us carrying a gun and a sack of

"We Did It! We Built the Bridge!"

goods, we were ready to move. Francis climbed on the mule, and the little monkey rode on Turk's back, making a thousand funny faces as he bounced along. All the other animals trailed behind us.

After our caravan crossed over Nonsuch Bridge, we passed through the high grass. The dogs lingered behind in the grass, howling loudly. Finally the older boys ran back to see what the trouble was.

"Father, come quickly!" Jack called. "Here is a monstrous porcupine!"

By the time I reached the spot, Turk and Flora were running frantically to and fro with bleeding noses. As they circled the frightened animal, the porcupine pierced them deeply once again with its sharp quills. This time they howled even louder.

Jack quickly took a pistol from his belt and shot the porcupine dead. The boys crowded around the extraordinary animal, hoping to drag it along with them. But unfortunately its

The Dogs Battle a Porcupine.

quills were too deadly, and they were forced to abandon it.

Not long afterward, we entered the place of the tall trees which had so intrigued Elizabeth.

"What trees! What height! What trunks!" I exclaimed. "I have never seen anything like them! This is indeed the place we shall make our home! Why, there's not an animal alive that could reach a house in those trees!"

Suddenly, Francis came running up. His mouth was crammed full of something as he called out, "Mother, Mother! Look at the wonderful fruit I have found!"

"For goodness sakes! You shouldn't eat anything unless you know what it is. You could be poisoned and die." With that, Elizabeth opened his mouth and removed the remains of a fig.

"A fig!" I cried. "Where did you get it?"

"In the grass, Papa, under these big trees, and there are many more. I thought they must be good to eat because all the animals are

"What Trees! What Height! What Trunks!"

eating them. Watch this." And Francis handed a fig to the little monkey, who turned it round and round, smelled it, and popped it right into his mouth.

"Bravo, Mr. Monkey!" cried Fritz and Jack.

"Now, boys," I said, "we must make a ladder that will reach the tall branches of our beautiful fig trees."

"Papa," said Ernest, "I saw some bamboo canes in a marsh near the shore. They'll make a fine ladder. Let's go get some."

Ernest, Fritz, and I set off for the shore. We cut the bamboo into five-foot-long pieces and tied them in a bundle.

Just as we were leaving to head for home, we heard a noise in the thicket. The boys and I jumped back, but Flora, who had accompanied us, pricked up her ears and dashed into the brush.

Before we knew what was happening, Flora was locked in deadly combat with a wild, screeching jungle animal.

Mr. Monkey Pops a Fig into His Mouth.

Flamingoes Spring Out.

CHAPTER 4

The House in the Trees

Our hearts were pounding as we crept nearer the thicket where Flora was trapped. With guns poised, we were ready to fire. Suddenly, a troop of large, pink flamingoes sprang out and with loud, rustling noises flew into the air.

"Flamingoes! Fritz shouted "Well, what do you know? They sounded more like baboons!"

Firing into the air, he shot down two of the large birds. One was quite dead; the other was merely wounded in one wing.

Unable to fly, the poor frightened bird darted toward the swamp, with Fritz following in close pursuit. Actually, it was Flora who reached the bird first and pinned it down until I arrived. The flamingo resisted my help strenuously, flapping its wings and twisting and turning, but I finally managed to grab hold of it.

Relieved that we had been spared an encounter with a more sinister creature, we set out for home. Ernest lugged the bamboo canes, and Fritz carried the dead flamingo, while I was in charge of the unhappy, squawking survivor.

"Come on, fellow, be still," I said to the flamingo once we were back at the giant trees. "I have some ointment that will ease your pain."

After treating the injury, I took a long string and tied the bird to a stake near the river so that it might go in and wash itself.

"The next order of business," I announced firmly to my family, "is to construct a ladder so that we can build a house in the trees. I

Setting Out for Home

am going to need everyone's help. So let's get to work."

"Ernest and I will be in charge of measuring the rope," volunteered Fritz.

"I have a job to do first," I answered.

Using triangles, I was able to determine the distance from the ground to the lowest tree branch. "It's forty feet," I called out, "so you will need eighty feet of rope for the two sides of your ladder."

While the boys were busy working on the ladder, I devised a scheme to hoist it up the tree when it was finished. By attaching the end of a ball of strong thread to a hollow bamboo reed filled with sand, I made an arrow-like device to toss over a tree limb. I even put a flamingo feather on the tip to help it fly straight. When my little invention deftly sailed over the branch and dangled down the other side, we all clapped our hands joyfully.

In the meantime, Fritz and Ernest were putting the finishing touches on the sturdy

Hoisting the Ladder up the Tree

ladder. Its sides were made of rope and its rungs were fashioned from sugar canes.

"What a great job you've done!" I said, stepping back to admire their handiwork.

I next tied the ladder to the end of the rope that hung down one side of the tree and yanked it up from the other side.

"Hurray! Hurray!" everyone cried as the ladder reached the desired branch and rested firmly upon it.

"Jack, you're the nimblest one of us. You go first," I told him.

While the rest of us held tightly to the end of the ladder, Jack scooted up the rungs with perfect ease.

"Father," he called down, "I'm not strong enough to tie the ladder to the tree."

"I can do it," said Fritz, and up he went.

In no time at all he had the ladder securely fastened to the branch. I followed next to attach a pulley to the tree trunk. By this means I planned to haul up the lumber for our house.

Fastening the Ladder to the Branch

THE SWISS FAMILY ROBINSON

The tree we had chosen was ideal, for its branches grew close together in a horizontal direction. On the first level we built a floor of wooden planks and around this platform we constructed a wall approximately four feet high, also made of planks.

We then hung our hammocks in boughs six feet above the floor. Then, throwing the sail-cloth over the higher branches that towered some 50 feet above the ground, we made a roof for our tree house. Working quickly, we pulled the cloth down and nailed it firmly to the wooden wall on two sides. The tree trunk formed the third side, and the front was left open to admit the fresh sea breeze. The house was beginning to look very impressive.

That night when we all gathered around a table that I built at the foot of the tree, Elizabeth brought out a large, earthen pot.

"The flamingo I killed!" exclaimed Fritz as his mother lifted the lid of the dish.

"Yes," answered Elizabeth, "I stewed it so

The House in the Tree

that it would be juicy and tender. After all, it was an old bird."

When we had devoured every morsel of the feast, we climbed the ladder to spend our first night in the tree-house. After everyone was safely inside, I pulled the ladder up behind me.

"How exciting!" cried Francis. "It's just like you drew up the drawbridge to our very own castle!"

"We will sleep well tonight, knowing we are safe from our enemies!" said Jack.

In the days that followed we did indeed feel as if the island were our own private kingdom. One morning at breakfast I said to my family, "What do you think of giving a name to our home and to the different parts of the island?"

"That's a wonderful idea!" said Ernest. "Where shall we start?"

"How about the bay where we first entered this country?"

"Why don't we call it Oyster Bay?" cried Fritz. "Remember all the oysters I found

Climbing the Ladder

there? That would be a perfect name."

"No, Lobster Bay," shouted Jack. "After all, that's where I discovered our first meal."

"By all rights it should be called Providence Bay," interrupted Elizabeth, "in gratitude to God for delivering us safely."

"Providence Bay it will be," I said.

And so it was decided. Tent House was the name selected for our first home and Falcon's Nest for our tree-house. We named the islet where we found the lumber for the bridge Shark Island to commemorate Fritz's courage in killing the sea monster. Flamingo Marsh was chosen for the swamp, Jackal's River for the stream that divided the island, and Family Bridge became the new name for Nonsuch Bridge.

Once we had made these decisions, we suddenly began to feel more at home. We spent days getting settled in the tree-house, transporting provisions over from Tent House, and exploring the island.

Transporting Provisions to Falcon's Nest

THE SWISS FAMILY ROBINSON

One morning Ernest and I went fishing in Providence Bay, where he caught a huge, fifteen-pound fish. As we started home, Flora dashed off after a strange animal, one which made the most extraordinary jumps imaginable. Thoughtlessly, Ernest lifted his gun and shot the creature dead.

"Look at him!" Ernest cried. "He's as large as a sheep, but he has the tail of a tiger. And his nose and hair are like a mouse's."

"You're right," I replied, "and his teeth are like a rabbit's, his front legs resemble those of a squirrel, and his hind legs are like stilts."

"Father," wailed Ernest, "I think I have just killed the most remarkable animal in the world. Whatever can he be?"

"Whatever Can He Be?"

Carrying the Kangaroo Home

CHAPTER 5

A Tortoise Takes Us for a Ride

"It's a kangaroo," I said. "To the best of my knowledge, however, kangaroos have never been seen anywhere other than on the coast of Australia. It was that famous explorer, Captain Cook, who originally discovered them."

"How are we going to get it home?" asked Ernest. "If we drag it on the ground, we'll spoil its beautiful skin."

"Why don't we tie its front legs together and carry it the rest of the way on these two canes here to the sled you boys made?" I suggested. And that is what we did.

Back at Falcon's Nest, we skinned the

kangaroo and cut its meat in pieces, some of which we planned to eat immediately, the rest we would salt and store for future use.

Elizabeth was delighted with the new supplies of food. "Your fish is magnificent," she said, praising Ernest's fifteen-pound catch. "We will certainly dine in splendor tonight."

Early the next morning, Fritz and I sailed back to the wreck to collect the last of the stores. The first thing we did was to make a large raft to help accommodate all our booty. Then we searched the ship and unearthed many unusual items that would be valuable to us as settlers in a new land. After all, the ship had originally been outfitted for that very purpose.

"Come here, Fritz," I called from the captain's cabin. "You won't believe what I have found."

"How beautiful!" cried Fritz as he ran to the chest at my feet and gazed down at the gold

"Your Fish Is Magnificent."

and silver watches, necklaces, and rings that the chest contained.

Once he got over his amazement, he tugged at my arm and cried, "Now, you must see what I discovered in a cask under the stairs."

I followed him to the cask and it was soon my turn to be amazed. "Why, there is every species of European fruit here!" I cried, as I peered in at the dozens of young plants that had been carefully packed in moss. "I see pear, plum, peach, apple, apricot, chestnut trees, and vine shoots."

"Are you going to plant them on the island?" Fritz asked.

"I most certainly am. Keep looking. There must be other things we can use."

And there were, including the pieces for a small sailing ship, which we planned to assemble and bring to shore on our next trip.

By the time we had finished, both the raft and the tub-boat were overflowing with supplies. At the last minute Fritz tossed in a

A Cask with Dozens of Young Plants

THE SWISS FAMILY ROBINSON

fishing net, the ship's compass, and two harpoons to which he had attached long ropes.

"I'm going to keep these in the bow," he said. "Then if we spot a big fish, we will be ready this time."

I nodded my approval, and we pushed out into the current, pulling our raft behind us with a strong rope. The sea was calm and the wind drew us gently along.

"There's something ahead," Fritz said. "Look through your telescope, Father, and tell me what it is."

"It's a tortoise!" I cried. "Why, he's fallen asleep in the sun right on top of the water."

"Steer close to him, so that we can take a good look at him."

As I changed our direction, Fritz's back was to me so I could not see what he was doing. Suddenly, there was a violent jerking of the boat and it began moving as fast as a speeding bullet through the water.

Alarmed now, I cried, "For heaven's sake,

Spotting a Tortoise

Fritz, what are you doing?"

"I speared him!" Fritz yened. "I speared him with my harpoon!"

Looking ahead, I saw that Fritz was right. The tortoise, wounded by the harpoon that had lodged in its flesh, was pulling us directly out to sea. As the boat moved faster and faster, my heart began to beat wildly. I grasped the sides of the boat and prayed.

When I looked up, I saw to my relief that the tortoise was headed straight toward our usual landing place. When we were almost there, the tide threw us up on a sand bank near the shore, and I stepped out of the boat to release the poor sea turtle. However, it suddenly plunged beneath the water and disappeared. Following the rope, I soon saw the tortoise stretched out across the white, sandy bottom. Knowing that the creature was in pain, I mercifully cut off its head with a hatchet and ended its suffering.

We ploughed our way through the water, the

A Wild Ride out to Sea

head of our sea prize on the muzzle of our gun.

"Hello! Hello!" Fritz called out as we neared the shore.

"What have we here?" cried Elizabeth as she and the younger boys rushed to greet us.

A tortoise, my dear, and one who has given me the fastest ride of my life. Is our sled handy so we can haul it up to Tent House?"

"Yes, it is. You can load it right on, along with some of the new provisions I see. "

Later that day, after we were settled, we flipped the tortoise on its back so that we could remove its shell and make use of the meat. Taking my hatchet, I separated the upper shell, which was round, from the bottom one, which was flat.

"Let me clean out the round shell," offered Fritz. "It will make an excellent bowl for washing clothes. "

"Fine idea. But let's not get so busy that we forget our last job on the wreck—bringing in the ship's boat we found in the hold."

An Excellent Bowl for Washing Clothes

THE SWISS FAMILY ROBINSON

"But it's in so many pieces, Father."

"Then we will have to put them together."

Every day for one week, we left early in the morning and returned to the island late at night. Finally, the sleek little sailing ship was ready, and we lowered her into the water.

The yacht had a small neat deck, several masts, billowing sails, and two small cannons nailed to the deck. As we approached shore, Fritz said, "Let's shoot off the cannon for Mother."

Elizabeth, Francis, and a very bewildered little monkey, his fingers in his ears, came down to inspect the ship.

"Come on, Mother, climb aboard," Fritz called, extending his hand. "We have decided to call our new ship *The Elizabeth.*"

"I'm touched," Elizabeth said, hugging us both. "We have accomplished a lot in the three weeks we have lived here. Now come see what I have done. Do I ever have a surprise for you!"

Shooting Off the Cannon

A Strange Procession up the Rocks

CHAPTER 6

The Journey into the Interior

What a strange procession we made as we wound our way up through the rocks to the waterfall that towered above Jackal's River. In the lead were Elizabeth and Francis, with Jack and Ernest close behind. Fritz and I brought up the rear, followed by a flock of stray ducks and geese who tagged along.

The little monkey, still keyed up from the cannon blast, ran ahead. Every now and then he'd stop and motion us on.

To my astonishment, Elizabeth led us to a handsome garden all laid out in neat little rows.

THE SWISS FAMILY ROBINSON

"I'm amazed," I said, "at all you have accomplished in such a short period of time. Was it hard work?"

"Not really," she answered, very pleased with herself. "The earth is light here and composed of many dead leaves. Francis and I found it easy to rake and hoe."

"Look, Papa!" cried Francis, pointing around him as he spoke. "We planted potatoes here, corn here, sugar cane here, and lettuce here. And over here we planted all the fruit trees."

"You haven't left anything for me to do," I said.

"Oh, yes, I have," Elizabeth assured me. "I'm going to depend on you to make an irrigation system using bamboo canes to carry the water over from the falls to our thirsty plants."

"This would be a good spot to house our pigeons and chickens," I said, looking around. "I could make individual coops from gourds

Francis Shows Off Mother's Garden.

and tie them in the trees."

"Maybe you could make hives for the bees," Elizabeth suggested.

"Father!" cried Ernest, who had wandered away. "Come quick! I found a crocodile!"

"A crocodile!" I said, laughing. "What an imagination you have, Ernest. Who ever heard of a crocodile living in these rocks without a drop of water?"

"See for yourself. He's asleep on that stone there."

We stole quietly to the ledge where the animal lay, but instead of a crocodile, it turned out to be a sort of lizard called an iguana.

"I'm going to shoot him," whispered Fritz.

"No, son. It would be hard to pierce that scaly coat. If you make him angry, he could be dangerous. I have a better idea."

I cut a stick from a bush and tied a long string to it. Then I knotted the loose end and cautiously tiptoed toward the iguana, who was snoozing peacefully in the sun. When I was

"Come Quick! I Found a Crocodile!"

very near to him, I began whistling a lively tune, an air from my native Switzerland.

The creature smiled in his sleep. Suddenly he opened one eye and raised his head to hear the music. As he looked all around, I tickled him gently with my stick.

To my joy the iguana flipped over, stretched himself flat on his back, and undulated with his tail, as if he was overwhelmed by the music. He raised his head again, and I threw my noose over him.

"Draw it tight! " cried Ernest.

"Strangle him!" yelled Jack.

"No!" I said firmly. "Why make him suffer any more than he has to?" And quick as a flash I plunged my knife into him. Soon he was dead.

Throwing the iguana over my shoulder, I started home to Falcon's Nest. Francis walked behind carrying the animal's tail which would have dragged the ground otherwise.

That night as we all sat under our fig tree

Tickling the Iguana Gently

dining on this new delicacy, I said, "I think the time has come to sink the wreck and explore the interior of the island. We have yet to see the land beyond the rocks at Tent House."

"Can I go this time?" begged Jack.

"Yes, I will need you three oldest boys to help blow up the ship too."

"When are we going to do that?" asked Fritz.

"Tomorrow. We will sail out to the wreck and put a cask of gunpowder on deck. Just before we abandon ship, we will light it. If luck is with us, we will be ashore before the explosion."

The actual destruction of the wreck was an emotional time for us all. As the ship sank into the sea, our hearts went with it. The question we were wondering was: Will we ever see our beloved Switzerland again?

That done, the hour came to set out on the expedition into the interior. Bidding Elizabeth

The Destruction of the Wreck

and Francis good-bye, we set out with Grizzle, our mule, who pulled our sled piled high with the necessary equipment—a tent, food, ammunition, and utensils. Turk and Flora came tearing after us.

The land beyond Tent House was equally as exotic as the side where we had settled. Our path led us through one forest after another of the most unusual trees we had ever seen. I recognized the guava tree, whose fruit resembled our apple, and the candleberry tree, whose heavy berries form candle wax when boiled.

"Your mother is going to be delighted with our discoveries," I told the boys as we roamed through some Indian rubber trees.

I left a large gourd under one of these trees to catch its milky sap. From this sap I would later make boots and shoes.

"My, these acorns are sweet," said Jack, tasting the nuts of the stately oaks.

"And the beans from these cocoa trees are

Father Points Out Many Trees.

good too", said Ernest, as he stuffed his pockets full. "They will make a delicious chocolate drink."

"You must come see this view," I called when we came out of the woods. In front of us was a magnificent bay that stretched far out to sea. "Now where is that Grizzle?"

"He just took off through the bamboo trees," Ernest said, "and he was going at a fast gallop too."

"Well, we must go after him," I answered.

But Grizzle was nowhere to be seen. Only his prints remained in the soil. An hour later we left the bamboo forest and came to a river, which we crossed. To our amazement we found the prints of other, much larger animals on the bank.

"What could they be?" asked Jack.

"Let's follow them and find out." I suggested.

Soon afterwards. we came to a great plain where we saw some tiny specks moving in the

Only Grizzle's Prints Remain.

distance. As we drew closer, we realized that they were animals the size of cows or horses.

"By George, they're wild buffaloes!" I exclaimed.

As we approached, the buffaloes remained motionless, merely staring at us with their large, round eyes. Those that were lying down rose lazily to their feet.

Suddenly, our fearless dogs ran into their midst and attacked a young buffalo. At that same moment I fired my gun, and the whole troop began to stampede. In no time at all they were out of sight.

Now we were left with only the young buffalo and his mother, whom I had wounded with my one shot. Angry now, she stomped her hoofs in the dust and bellowed loudly. With her head held low and steam pouring from her nostrils, she took aim and charged directly at Turk and Flora!

"They're Wild Buffaloes!"

Firing at the Enraged Buffalo

CHAPTER 7

Grizzle's Strange Companion

Watching the enraged female buffalo gallop toward Turk and Flora, I realized they would be torn to pieces in minutes. Quickly, I raised my double-barreled gun and fired. The buffalo fell dead only a few feet away from the terrified dogs.

"Good shooting, Father!" cried Ernest, as the boys rushed forward to observe the slain animal. "Now, are you going to kill the little buffalo too?"

"No," I said. "With Grizzle lost and probably gone for good, I will need this fellow to take his place. Come help me tie his legs."

This done, I next took a pocket knife and cut a small hole in the buffalo's nostrils into which I inserted a string. Naturally, the creature was furious. However, the pain in his nose and the rope around his legs prevented him from running away. The first time I pulled the cord, I saw that my prisoner was docile and ready for the long march home.

Our entry into camp was a triumphant one indeed. Elizabeth and Francis could hardly believe their eyes as we strutted in proudly with the shaggy buffalo. On Fritz's shoulders sat two beautiful birds he had captured on the homeward trail. One was a green parrot and the other, a Malabar eagle, which he had blindfolded to prevent it from attacking anyone.

"What a trip you've had! " exclaimed Elizabeth. "But surely acquiring this buffalo is your greatest accomplishment!"

"Papa, Papa!" cried Francis, running alongside the buffalo. "What are you going to do with him?"

A Triumphant Entry into Camp

"Right now I'm going to tie him up with the cow and see how they get along."

"Maybe we should feed him first," Jack suggested, as he handed the newcomer some milk and sliced roots.

Greedily, the buffalo devoured it all and began to browse peacefully next to the cow.

"Fritz, where are you going to put your birds?" Ernest asked.

"Over here," Fritz answered. And he fastened both the parrot and the eagle to the same tree root, but foolishly removed the blindfold from the eagle's eyes. The eagle flew into a rage and killed the poor parrot.

"Bad bird!" Fritz screamed. "I'm going to break that neck of yours! "

"Wait," Ernest cried. "You can always find another parrot, but never such a magnificent hunter as this eagle. Properly trained, it will be able to catch many birds for us. Let me have it and it will soon be as submissive as a new puppy."

Milk and Roots for the Buffalo

THE SWISS FAMILY ROBINSON

With that, Ernest lit up a pipe and began to blow the tobacco smoke into the eagle's face. "This is an old trick used by the Carib Indians," he told us. "Once their eagles became senseless from the smoke, the Indians were able to tame them."

"You've killed him" yelled Fritz, as the bird stood motionless on his perch.

"How could he be dead and still be stand ing?" Ernest retorted. "He'll come out of the trance in a minute."

And Ernest was right. Soon the bird opened its eyes and looked at us in surprise. Its anger was gone and in only a few days it was tame.

Amazingly enough, we were able to repeat this same procedure not long afterwards. Elizabeth, feeling that the rope ladder was dangerous, urged me to build a set of winding stairs inside the hollow tree trunk. When I first chopped into the tree, hundreds of bees swarmed out, buzzing menacingly, and stinging the children.

Ernest Tries an Indian Trick.

"Why not try putting the bees in a stupor like we did with the eagle?" Fritz suggested.

"Alright," I said.

The scheme worked beautifully. Once the bees were asleep, we cut their combs loose and put them into some gourds which we nailed to a nearby tree. The bees had two brand-new hives. We had an abundant supply of delicious honey, and in a month's time Elizabeth had her winding stairs.

It was a time of great prosperity at Falcon's Nest. Elizabeth spent her days at a handsome loom, weaving cloth from the fibers of the flax plants we discovered. The boys and I were busy planting crops and constructing a fountain.

We even built a stable to house our growing family of animals. The pig had given birth to a litter of seven piglets. The hens had produced forty chicks; the goats, two kids; and the sheep, five lambs. To top it all off, Flora was now the mother of six newborn puppies.

Winding Stairs for Mother

Then one day we had still another stroke of luck. We were just nailing the door of the captain's cabin onto the tree opening of the winding stairs when we heard a terrible howling in the distance. Collecting our guns, we all ran to see what was the cause of the disturbance.

"Why, it's Grizzle!" Fritz called. "He's coming home!"

The mule moved toward us leisurely, stopping every now and then to nibble some grass.

"What is that with him?" asked Francis.

" I think it' s an onagra, " I said.

"What's an onagra?"

"A wild donkey," I explained. "They travel in herds on the hot, dry plains of western Asia. Look at those yellow patches on each thigh."

" And that black stripe down his back," added Jack.

"And look at that funny tail, with the fuzzy tuft of hair on the end of it!" exclaimed Ernest.

The two animals were very close to us now.

Grizzle Brings Home an Onagra.

Fritz, holding a noose in his hand, moved softly forward and offered Grizzle some oats. As the wild donkey saw his companion gobble up this strange food, he edged closer. At that point, Fritz threw the noose over his head. The onagra was ours!

Everyone clapped their hands and danced for joy.

"Now, boys," I said, "we must try to tame and train him just as we did the buffalo. It's not going to be easy, so I hope you are ready for a real challenge."

A Noose over the Onagra's Head

The Onagra's First Rider

CHAPTER 8

The Grotto That Time Forgot

The beautiful female onagra soon became our most prized possession. The boys were amazed to learn her coat would change from cinnamon to pale yellow-brown during the rainy season. We all agreed that she was the most unusual animal of her species we'd ever seen.

Her training was, as I had expected, a tedious undertaking. Knipps, our monkey, was her first rider. He stuck so tightly to her back that in spite of the onagra's plunging and kicking, he was not thrown.

"Let me try now," begged Francis. "After all,

THE SWISS FAMILY ROBINSON

I'm the smallest one in the family."

Although I gave my consent, I was careful to lead the donkey with a halter so that no harm would come to my son.

"I'm next," insisted Jack. But he landed, only a few minutes later, unhurt in the sand.

Ernest, Fritz, and I followed suit, but we were soon dizzy and exhausted from the frantic galloping. Fritz, however, didn't give up. Over and over again he mounted the wild donkey and rode off. Finally, the onagra got accustomed to us and was quite tame.

We chose the name Lightfoot for her because of her incredible strength and swiftness. To this day, I can still picture Fritz on the back of Lightfoot as they tore up and down the beach with the speed of lightning.

This pleasant way of life ended abruptly with the arrival of the rainy season, which was our winter. The rain fell in such heavy torrents that it turned the entire countryside into one big lake.

Running with the Speed of Lightning

THE SWISS FAMILY ROBINSON

The winds blew so furiously that they deluged our beds with rain and threatened to carry us away. We had no choice but to move from the tree-house into the stable that we had built between the roots below.

Crowded together in the dark, we were nearly sick from the foul odor of the livestock. In addition, we were stifled by smoke whenever we kindled a fire and drenched with rain when we opened the doors. Week after week, we were prisoners inside the barn.

For the first time, Elizabeth was obviously upset. "We simply will have to build another winter home elsewhere," she stated.

"You're right," I replied. "I don't think any of us could go through this again."

"We could still use the tree-house for a summer residence," she went on. "After all, we all do love it there."

"Agreed, my dear."

"Listen to this," Fritz said as he leafed through a book he found in the bottom of a

Prisoners Inside the Barn

THE SWISS FAMILY ROBINSON

chest. "Robinson Crusoe cut his home out of solid rock. Why can't we do the same thing?"

"We can," Ernest said. "How about the rocks on the other side of the island? They just might suit our purpose."

As soon as the gloomy weeks of rain had ended and we had gotten Falcon's Nest in order, we set out to investigate the rocks behind Tent House. Here we found that the ravages of winter weather had taken their toll too.

The winds and rain had beaten down the tent and scattered our provisions hither and yon. Luckily our sailing boat was still in anchor, but the tub-boat was completely shattered.

"I will certainly be glad when we have more solid winter quarters," I told the boys.

"We had better get right to work," said Fritz.

I had to confess to the boys that I had my doubts about carving a home out of those

The Storm Has Taken Its Toll.

rocks. "However," I added, "I'm willing to give it a try."

Wielding pick-axes, chisels, hammers, and iron levers, we set to work at an enchanting spot that faced Providence Bay, Jackal's River, and Family Bridge. With charcoal, I marked the opening we wished to make, and the boys then began hammering away. At first, the progress was monotonous and slow, but as we advanced, the rock became softer. When we had cut into it about a foot, we were able to loosen the rock with a spade, just as if it were dried mud.

After several days of hard work, we had penetrated seven feet into the rock. Then, one day as Fritz was carting out a wheelbarrow full of rock and dirt, Jack cried out, "Father, we have pierced through all the way! Come see!"

The boys lit some candles and, holding them high, we advanced forward in one solemn procession.

Seven Feet into the Rock

The most beautiful and magnificent spectacle awaited us. Our candles illuminated a large grotto whose sides sparkled in the flickering light like a sea of diamonds. Hundreds of crystals of every length and shape hung from the top of the cavern and joined with those on the bottom and sides to form pillars, altars, and a variety of other figures.

"It's like the palace of a great European king! " cried Fritz.

"Or the temple of a Roman God!" added Jack.

"One thing is certain," I told them. "No man has ever set foot here before. It has been hidden away from civilization since time began."

"What do you think this is, Father?" asked Ernest, breaking off one of the crystals that hung down from the ceiling.

"It's salt!" I exclaimed in delight. "Boys, we have discovered a salt mine!"

"Will we still be able to live here?" asked

A Magnificent Grotto!

THE SWISS FAMILY ROBINSON

Fritz anxiously. "I mean, with the salt?"

"Of course we will," I answered. "If you notice, the floor is level and covered with a fine, white sand. The cavern itself is tight and dry. Why, it's the perfect site for our winter home."

However, we continued to live at Falcon's Nest for many months. During this time, we converted the grotto into a comfortable residence that would house not only our family, but our growing brood of animals as well.

On one side we constructed a stable and a workroom that would accommodate the livestock, their feed, and all our provisions and equipment.

On the other side was our home, which consisted of a bedroom for Elizabeth and myself, a bedroom for the boys, a dining room, and a kitchen. Here, we built a fireplace and a chimney that extended through the roof. With the exception of the dining room, each room

A Comfortable New Home

had a window which we chiseled out of the rock. *"Felsenheim,"* or "The Dwelling in the Rock, was the name of our new home. We soon realized that we had made a smart move, for the surrounding area was full of an endless supply of fish and game. Immense turtles visited the shore to deposit their eggs and schools of salmon and sturgeon swelled the bay. Large cranes, flying through the corn fields, were frequently captured by Fritz's sharp-eyed eagle, while kangaroos were seen jumping in and out of the sugar cane.

One afternoon as we wandered through the woods, we came upon a grove of bushes that appeared to be covered with snowflakes. Fritz darted into them on Lightfoot and returned with his hands full of the fluffy tufts.

"Father," he cried, "is this what I think is?"

"Is This What I Think It Is?"

"Let's Bring Home All We Can."

CHAPTER 9

A Holiday...Then Horror!

I examined the soft, fluffy balls that Fritz handed me, then announced, "Why, it's cotton."

"Cotton!" exclaimed Francis. "What's cotton?"

"It's a plant from which most of our clothes are made," Fritz told him with great authority.

"Come," I said to Elizabeth. "Take a look. This discovery is going to make life here a lot easier."

"Indeed it will," she answered. "Let's bring home all we can."

THE SWISS FAMILY ROBINSON

The ripe pods had burst open, and the wind had scattered their contents over the ground. Some of the white fluff had gathered on the bushes, while the rest floated gently in the air.

Working quickly, we collected as much cotton as our bags would hold. In the meantime, Elizabeth filled her pockets with seeds to plant in her garden above Tent House.

"You know," I said as we trudged homeward, "this is an important occasion, not just because we discovered cotton, but for another reason too. According to my calculations, tomorrow will be our second anniversary on the island."

"Is this really true?" Elizabeth asked. "I can hardly believe so much time has passed."

"It is true, my dear. Think of all the adventures we have had and how good God has been to us. I am going to declare tomorrow holiday—a special day of celebration."

"You mean we are going to have a party?"

Collecting the Cotton in Bags

cried Francis, jumping for joy. "Oh, I can hardly wait!"

Actually, Francis didn't have long to wait, for when the morning dawned, Elizabeth and I had the entire day's festivities planned. Greeting my sons on the lawn beneath Falcon's Nest, I said, "You boys have been practicing wrestling, running, swimming, shooting, and horseback riding here on the island for the past two years. Now we are going to see who are the champions of these various feats."

And so the competitions began, with Elizabeth cheering the boys on and Turk and Flora running alongside them. Unquestionably, the highlight of the day was the horseback-riding event.

Fritz mounted Lightfoot and Ernest rode Grizzle, but they were no match for Jack's skillful handling of the wild buffalo. A practiced groom could not have managed a thoroughbred horse with more grace and ease.

The Horseback Riding Event

"Jack, my boy," I boomed out, "I hereby declare you the winner of this contest."

"No, Papa." interrupted Francis. "You haven't seen what I can do yet."

And into the arena rode Francis, mounted on his young buffalo bull, Broumm, who was only four months old.

Elizabeth had made a saddle of kangaroo skin and stirrups that adjusted to Francis's little legs. There he sat, a whip in his right hand, and his animal's bridle in his left hand.

With his brothers urging him on, Francis proceeded to maneuver his steed beautifully. Around and around the ring they went with the buffalo obeying instructions to the letter.

"Francis," I said, "I'm really proud of you. What an expert horseman you have become!"

When the contests were over, we hurried to the grotto, which was ablaze with torches. Elizabeth, as Queen of the Day, was seated in a special elevated chair decorated with flowers. As I called the boys forward to receive

Francis Maneuvers the Young Bull.

their prizes, she gave each one a kiss on the forehead.

"Fritz," I began, "you are our champion swimmer and expert shot. This English rifle and hunting knife are your rewards."

"Thank you, Father," he said, coming forward to claim his prizes. "I shall always cherish them as a remembrance of this day."

"Ernest," I continued, "you are, without a doubt, our best runner. Please accept this gold watch for your own. And, Jack, these steel spurs are yours for your outstanding horsemanship."

"Thank you, Father," they both said with big grins.

"Now, Francis, I haven't forgotten you," I assured him. "For your skill in riding your buffalo, I present you with these new stirrups and a box of colors. Congratulations, son!"

"Thank you, Papa," he said, shaking my hand firmly. "This is the best holiday I have ever had."

Prizes for the Boys

Turning to Elizabeth, I slipped my arm around her waist. "My dear, this sewing box is my gift to you to thank you for all your courage and support during the last two years."

There were tears in her eyes as Elizabeth opened the box and fingered the needles, thread, and scissors inside. "Thank you," she whispered. "I think this has been my favorite holiday too."

And so our day of celebration ended on a very happy note.

The next morning, we were all back at work, since we were well aware that the rainy season was close at hand. For safety's sake, we usually worked in pairs. However, at noontime, Jack mounted Grizzle and rode off alone to Flamingo Marsh. Here, he hoped to find some thin willow twigs with which to build nests for our pigeons.

As he reached the outskirts of the swamp, he heard nothing but the mournful cry of a

"Thank You."

whipporwill. He proceeded in slowly on foot, stopping occasionally to examine the rushes. To his dismay they were much too thick to cut.

Deeper and deeper into the swamp Jack went. Suddenly, he came to a spot that was a mass of soft, black mud. "Oh dear!" he muttered to himself. "This isn't the way I want to go." And as he turned to retrace his steps, his feet slipped, and he fell into the mud. Before he knew what was happening, he was up to his knees in the wet mud and sinking faster.

"Quicksand!" he shouted. "Help! Oh, somebody help me!"

"Quicksand! Somebody Help Me!"

Willow Twigs Buoy Up Jack.

CHAPTER 10

Terror at Felsenheim

As Jack slowly sank into the quicksand, only Grizzle heard his frantic cries for help. The poor bewildered mule came running to the edge of the marsh, where he stood braying loudly.

Realizing now that no one could hear him beyond the dense wall of willow trees that surrounded him, Jack made one last effort to save himself. Twisting and turning, he managed to get his knife out of his pocket and cut two large bundles of willow twigs. These he wedged under his arms. Miraculously, they buoyed him up so that he was actually able to make some headway toward dry ground.

He whistled softly to Grizzle, who inched closer and closer. Then, Jack grabbed the mule's tail and clung for dear life. As Grizzle tugged and pulled, Jack felt himself being carried forward. In a matter of minutes, he was on safe ground.

As Jack staggered into camp an hour later, I asked him, "Where have you been to get so dirty?"

"Flamingo Marsh."

"What on earth were you doing there alone?" I demanded angrily.

"I wanted to surprise Mother and make some nests for her pigeons. I went there to get these willows," he said, tossing down the muddy reeds. "But they're too thick, I'm afraid. The worst thing was that I fell in the quicksand. I escaped just in the knick of time."

"Oh, Jack!" Elizabeth cried, rushing up to Jack and embracing him. "Thank heaven

Grizzle Pulls Jack to Safe Ground.

you're safe. Now promise us you won't undertake any expeditions alone again."

"I promise, Mother," Jack replied sheepishly. "I'm sorry if I worried you."

"See that you remember that promise," she said firmly. "At least we can use these twigs to make baskets in which to carry our grain. Now, the first thing you must do is to get out of those muddy clothes and take a bath in the river."

"Better make it snappy," I added to Jack. "There is still much work to be done before we officially move into *Felsenheim*."

The major problem we faced was that of lighting the grotto. Except for three rooms which had windows, the cave was in complete darkness. Finally, I hit upon a scheme. I took a bamboo pole that was the same height as the grotto and planted it in the ground. I then gave Jack a hammer, a pulley, and a rope and asked him to make the pole steady.

In a moment, he was at the top, driving the

Jack Makes a Promise.

pulley right into the ceiling. He pulled the cord over it and jumped agilely to the ground. I then tied one end of the cord to a large lantern from the ship and raised it to the top. Once the; lantern was lighted, the whole cavern was aglow.

"What a beautiful sight!" Elizabeth ex claimed. "It's amazing how the sides of the cave reflect the light!"

"It's like broad daylight now. Good thinking on your part, Papa," Jack chimed in.

While Jack and I put the finishing touches on the workroom, Ernest and Francis took charge of arranging the shelves in the library. Besides the Bible, the ship had contained books on history, botany, voyages, and travel. We had also found maps, a globe, and dictionaries from other lands.

We all knew a little French, for this was spoken as much as German was in our native Switzerland. In addition, I encouraged my sons to master the English language. My

Arranging the Shelves

inspection of the maps and charts had led me to believe we were somewhere near Malaysia, so I struggled to learn the Malay tongue.

As our work at *Felsenheim* neared completion, we saw black clouds gathering on the horizon. Lightning flashed and thunder roared. Winds swept over the coast, billowing waves rose, and for fifteen days we had the worst storm anyone could ever imagine.

However, we were happy and secure inside our grotto. What would have become of us in our tree-house at Falcon's Nest? And how could we have withstood the storm in our tent?

At last the rain stopped, and we ventured out again.

Fritz, whose eagle eye had led him to make most of our discoveries, suddenly cried out, "Father, come look! There's a strange animal on the other side of the river, near Falcon's Nest. And it's coming this way."

"What do you think it is?" Elizabeth asked,

The Worst Storm Imaginable!

running up to me.

"I've never seen anything like it before," Fritz said in awe. "First it moves forward, rolling itself up into large rings. Then, it stops and unrolls itself again. It stops; it starts. And then it marches on once more, but I can't see either its feet or its legs."

"Here, Papa, look through this," Ernest said, handing me my spyglass.

Pointing it in the direction of Falcon's Nest, I shouted, "Why, it's a huge serpent—dark greenish-blue in color. It must be all of fourteen feet long. Hurry, Francis! Hurry, everyone! Run back to the grotto as fast as you can! It's a boa constrictor!"

Once inside *Felsenheim,* we bolted the door,. barricaded the windows, and waited in silence for the arrival of our enemy. When it was about thirty paces away, it stopped as if it sensed our presence. Ernest pushed his gun through the door and fired. Jack, Francis, and Elizabeth followed his example.

Seeing a Serpent Through the Spyglass

Although the monster raised its head and fell back, the shots did not even penetrate its scales. Fritz and I then fired in rapid succession, but it was useless. While we all watched in stunned disbelief, the boa constrictor slithered away toward the marsh where our ducks and geese lived.

"What are we going to do?" cried Fritz. "We are powerless to kill him!"

"I'm afraid we have no choice but to remain inside the grotto. No one is to open even the door—that's an order!"

For three long days and nights, we maintained our vigil at *Felsenheim. Our* position was a dangerous one. We knew that the boa constrictor was still inside the marsh because of the unrest among the fowl. Yet an attack upon it by my family might cost a life. On the other hand, none of the animals would stand a chance against it. To make matters worse, our animals' fodder was nearly gone.

Finally I said to Fritz, "You attach the

Useless Firing

animals together with a strong rope and lead them across the river to graze. I will post myself on a rock above the swamp and keep an eye on the serpent. Elizabeth, you must be in charge of the door."

Unfortunately, Elizabeth didn't wait for my signal and opened the door before the animals were securely tied together. No sooner did Grizzle see a ray of light than he shot out the door like an arrow.

"Come back, Grizzle!" we called, but he never stopped.

He headed straight for the marsh and we watched in horror as the snake rose up and shot out its long, forked tongue!

Grizzle Heads For the Marsh.

The Boa Constrictor Crushes Grizzle.

CHAPTER 11

The Mirage in the Desert

Grizzle soon saw the terrible danger that awaited him in the marsh. He immediately began to run the other way, braying with all his might. But neither his cries nor his legs could save him from the deadly enemy. In a flash, the boa constrictor reached out and crushed him in its monstrous rings.

"Oh, how terrible!" Elizabeth wailed, turning away from the window. "What can we do to save poor Grizzle?"

"Quick, Father!" yelled Fritz. "Shoot the snake!"

"I can't," I replied. "For if I fail to kill him

and merely wound him, he might attack us. It's a chance I simply cannot take."

Just then, we heard Grizzle's bones cracking as the monster swallowed him in one big gulp. To our amazement, the boa completely lost its strength and slumped down in a stupor.

"At last," I said, "he is in our power. Fire, Fritz! "

Fritz and I fired together, but we didn't kill the serpent. Instead it raised its head and glared at us with fire in its eyes. We moved closer, aimed at its eyes, and fired again. A slight quiver ran through the boa's body, and it soon lay dead upon the sand before us, stretched out like the mast of a ship.

"Thank God that is over," Elizabeth said heaving a sigh of relief.

"We have nothing more to fear from him now," I declared, putting my arm around my trembling wife. "But he may have a mate hiding nearby."

"Or a nest of babies," said Francis.

Dead on the Sand

"Then, we'd really be in trouble," moaned Fritz.

"I think we should check out those possibilities," I said. "We will search through the marsh first, then spread out and cover the region around Falcon's Nest."

Trooping through the marsh, we easily recognized traces of the boa, for the rushes were bent down and broken where it had passed through, and there were deep spiral impressions in the wet ground where it had rested its enormous rings. But we found no signs of a companion or a nest of eggs or little ones.

At the border of the swamp, Ernest suddenly cried out, "Come quickly! I have just killed a young boa."

"That's not a boa, Ernest," I told him as reached his side. "It's an eel."

It was, indeed, a superb eel, approximately four feet long. Ernest had walked straight up to it, hit it several times on the head with his

"Come Quickly!"

gun with as much courage as it would have taken to kill a dozen boa constrictors.

"We'll take it home with us," I said. "It'll make a fine meal another day."

As we circled the countryside around our tree-house, we saw fewer and fewer traces of the serpent. Satisfied that we were safe now, we returned to *Felsenheim*.

Before we had gone off, Fritz had left a pig roasting in a trench, which he had filled with red hot pebbles and covered with a layer of bark and earth. Now, as he pulled back the covering, the most delicious odor drifted up through the air.

"Oh, something smells good!" exclaimed Francis.

"This is simply marvelous!" raved Elizabeth, as she took her first bite of the stuffing of potatoes and roots that Fritz had made.

"Yes, my boy," I added, "you are quite a cook. Congratulations on a job well done."

"What are we going to do now, Papa?" asked

"Oh, Something Smells Good!"

Jack. "After all, we are well settled in the grotto, and the boa's reign of terror is over. "

"It has occurred to me that we should make another trip into the interior of the island. Do you realize that we have lived here three years without exploring everything?"

"Three years!" the boys cried in amazement.

"That's hard to believe," quipped Elizabeth.

"When do you want to leave for the trip?"

"Would tomorrow morning suit everyone?"

The family was agreeable, and as soon as the sun came peeking over the horizon at dawn, we set out for the land beyond the rocks. After two hours, I gave the signal to halt.

We were high on a hill overlooking a wide sandy plain and surrounded on all sides by a pine forest. We investigated the woods, but discovered nothing except two wild cats who fled into the trees before we could aim our guns at them.

We set up camp and left Elizabeth and

Two Wild Cats Flee into the Trees.

THE SWISS FAMILY ROBINSON

Francis there while the rest of us forged across the plain. "This is where we saw the buffaloes the time before," Jack pointed out.

"My, it's hot!" complained Ernest. "May I have a drink of water, Father?"

But the water in the gourds had become so warm, we were unable to drink it. The sun beat down on our heads, and the sand burned our feet. We were in a vast desert that stretched in all directions as far as the eye could see.

After several hours, we arrived at a huge rock that afforded us some refuge from the sun. Exhausted, we leaned against the sides, sucking on some bits of sugar cane that I had brought along for just such an emergency.

"What is that I see?" cried Fritz suddenly. "Look there, in the distance. There are three horsemen galloping toward us. They must be Arabs of the desert!"

"Arabs!" said Ernest. "Bedouins, you mean!"

"Bedouins are part of the great family of

A Vast Desert!

Arabs," I explained, "so Fritz is right. Take my spyglass, Ernest, and tell us what you see."

"Oh, I see wagons loaded with hay!" he said, "but they are so far away I can't tell much about them."

"Let me see!" cried Jack, grabbing the glass. "Oh, I see cavaliers carrying lances with a banner on each point."

"Now I'm going to take a look," I said. "I want to see for myself." I put the glass to my eye, then chuckled. "Well, your Arabs, your cavaliers, your hay carts are not those things at all. You have all merely seen a mirage."

"A mirage!" Jack cried. "What is a mirage?"

"A mirage is an image caused by the reflection of light in such a way that something far away seems to be near and often looks like something else. What you really see are three ostriches traveling together. Quick! Let's hide

Seeing a Mirage

and take them by surprise."

We all crouched down behind some plants that grew on the rock and waited until the ostriches stopped right before us. When they became aware of our presence, they hesitated for a minute. Then, the dogs, which we could not keep quiet, sprang out at them. And away flew the timid birds.

"Send your eagle after them, Fritz," I commanded.

Fritz removed the hood from the eagle's head and threw the bird up in the air. The eagle quickly lit upon the head of the male ostrich, which we recognized by its beautiful white tail feathers. Attacking its eyes, the eagle brought the ostrich to the ground with a thud. As we rushed up, we saw that the big bird was dead.

"What a pity!" Fritz said. "He would have looked so grand strutting among our animals."

"Hurry over here!" cried Jack. "I've found an

The Eagle Attacks the Ostriches.

ostrich nest with thirty eggs in it. Let's take them home and hatch them."

"Impossible!" said Fritz. "Why, each egg weighs three pounds. There is no way we could carry them across the desert."

"Then, we shall have to return another time," said Jack. "For now, each of us can take one egg. That's the solution."

As we trooped home we saw herds of buffalo, monkeys, and antelope in the distance. Finally, we came to an oasis with green grass and clear, cold water. "We will call this lovely spot Green Valley," I said.

As we rested and refreshed ourselves, we suddenly heard two horrible howls and a cry of distress from Ernest, who had wandered ahead. A moment later he appeared, running toward us at full speed, his face deadly white.

"Bears! Bears!" he screamed. "They are following me!" And the poor boy fell in my arms more dead than alive.

Each Person Carries an Ostrich Egg.

"Prepare To Fire!"

CHAPTER 12

Capturing the World's Biggest Bird

Shivers ran up and down my spine as I watched two enormous brown bears stagger toward me. "Keep still, boys," I whispered. "Prepare to fire."

Fritz, with courage far beyond his years, took his place beside me. Behind us Jack raised his gun, while Ernest, who had dropped his weapon in his terror, ran away.

"Fire!" I cried, and we all fired together.

Although we did not kill the bears, we broke the jaw of one and fractured the shoulder of the other. Turk and Flora, barking loudly, charged them. Soon the four were rolling in the dust, and the bears' blood poured in streams upon the sand.

"Be careful not to shoot the dogs," I cautioned. "But move in as close as you can. Aim right at the bears' heads and shoot to kill. Now, fire!"

This time, our teamwork was successful. The huge animals reared back on their hind legs, uttered one agonizing cry, and fell dead.

We devoted most of the next day to skinning the bears and preserving their meat, which we smoked and stored for use during the rainy season.

We then collected about one hundred pounds of grease and stored it in bamboo canes to use for cooking or on bread in place of butter. The bears' carcasses we tossed to the dogs, who ravenously picked the bones clean. Our last chore was to clean the soft, furry skins, which we presented to Elizabeth to use as coverlets for our beds or as rugs before our roaring fires at night.

Presenting the Skins to Elizabeth

Looking up from the pile of skins, I said "I'm afraid this has been tedious work. Why don't you boys relax and afterwards make your own expedition into the desert?"

"Good idea!" said Jack and Fritz. "Maybe we could catch some of those antelope we saw before."

"Count me out," said Ernest. "Those bears really exhausted me."

"Let me go too!" begged Francis.

And so it was decided. Jack and Francis rode off on our buffalo, whom we called Storm, and Fritz was mounted on Lightfoot.

Elizabeth and I watched as they rode out of camp, then we began the clean-up detail. As evening approached, we gathered around our hearth, where Elizabeth was cooking two bears' paws. Just as we were about to sit down to eat, the boys came in from hunting.

"We had a great chase, Papa!" cried Jack.

"Look at these magnificent Angora rabbits and the beautiful cuckoo bird that Fritz's eagle

Bringing Home Angora Rabbits

captured for us!"

"That's not all," added Fritz. "We have taken a whole troop of antelope prisoners. I thought we could take all our new animals to Shark Island, where they can run loose. Then, we can hunt and tame them whenever we please."

"I'm certainly glad to hear that," said E,lizabeth, petting the fluffy, white rabbits "Otherwise, these two will eat all the vegetables in my garden."

"As the rabbits multiply, they will furnish us many a tasty meal and many a warm, fur hat," I said. "Say, did you boys pass by the ostrich' s nest by any chance?"

"No, Papa, we didn't get that far today, Fritz said.

"Then, I think we'd better go back tomorrow. I need to collect more sap from the rubber tree anyway."

The next morning, we set off on Lightfoot and her young colt, Rapid, who had joined our

A Troop of Antelope

little family only months before. We passed through Green Valley and made our way across the sand to the giant rock which we now called Arab's Tower.

When we reached the nest, we saw four ostriches, three females and a male, rise and come toward us. This time, Fritz had muzzled the dogs and taped the eagle's beak shut so that they would not kill the birds.

I seized a long string with balls on the end of it and twirling it over my head, lassoed the male ostrich. Unfortunately, I only succeeded in pinning his wings to his sides. The frightened bird turned round and round, using his long legs in a frantic effort to escape. At this, point Fritz released his eagle who pounced upon the ostrich and lifted him up in the air. Jack threw the string so skillfully that the bird fell helplessly to the ground.

"Hurray! Hurray!" the boys shouted in great joy, pleased to have finally captured the biggest bird in the world.

Lassoing the Ostrich

THE SWISS FAMILY ROBINSON

The ostrich's arrival at *Felsenheim* was a time of great excitement. At first he was quite violent, pecking everyone who touched him and refusing to eat. Then, Elizabeth made some tidbits of corn and butter, which we poked down his throat. He loved them, and from that time on he ate everything in sight.

In the weeks to come, we tamed him and taught him to carry a rider. Soon, he and the boys were galloping all over the island.

We had brought back, along with a new supply of sap from the rubber tree, six ostrich eggs. These were placed in an artificial nest of cotton and put in the oven. In time, three of them actually hatched. But they were the drollest looking birds we had ever seen. They looked more like fuzzy ducks walking on stilts than ostriches. However, we fed them well and took good care of them. We used their shells for elegant vases, which I put on large wooden pedestals. Elizabeth kept them filled with fragrant flowers.

The Ostrich Pecks Everyone.

"Our Ostrich Is a Splendid Horse!"

CHAPTER 13

The Cajack

One morning at breakfast, Fritz said, "Our big ostrich is a splendid horse. We also have a sled to transport our provisions and a ship and canoe anchored in Providence Bay. Now we need a boat that will glide over the water like an ostrich does on land. I have something very unique in mind, but I can't make it alone. Are each of you willing to help me?"

"First, you must tell us your idea," I said, "and then we will vote whether or not to make it a family project."

As Elizabeth cleared away the dishes from

the breakfast table, Fritz outlined his plan. "I have read that the people of Greenland have a vessel that skims lightly over the water. They call it a cajack. I see no reason why we can't make one ourselves.

"What is this cajack like?" asked Jack.

"Well, it's sort of a canoe in the form of a shell," Fritz explained. "It's so light that you carry it on your shoulders once you have reached land."

"The idea certainly has merit," I said. "What materials would you use?"

"The Greenlanders use walrus skins for the body of the boat, but we could substitute seal skins. Strips of whalebone, bamboo canes, and rushes will make up the sides and give it form."

"It sounds like a great idea!" I exclaimed. I hearby vote that we begin construction on Fritz's proposed cajack this very day."

"I second the motion," said Ernest.

"Me too," piped up Francis.

Fritz Outlines His Plan.

THE SWISS FAMILY ROBINSON

With all five of us working, we had the skeleton of the cajack ready the next day. We then covered the interior with a coat of gum and moss and pulled the seal skins down over the outside. We sewed them together in the middle where they met and coated the outside with gum elastic to keep out the water.

While I fashioned oars from bamboo poles, Elizabeth made Fritz a special airtight suit that molded him from head to toe. The outfit was made of linen, prepared with a solution of India rubber. The seams were coated with a thick gum, made from the dried juices of tropical plants, that stretched easily and did not allow water to seep in. Fritz was given a pipe that he could use for breathing when swimming underwater.

Our first reaction when we finally saw Fritz dressed in his suit was to burst out laughing. But he gravely plunged in the water and struck out for Shark Island. We followed in the cajack and arrived at the same time.

The Cajack Takes Shape.

"My outfit worked beautifully," Fritz cried triumphantly as he removed the hood. "See - there's not a drop of water inside."

"Now Mother will have to make each of us suit like that," Jack said.

That trip to Shark Island was very successful. We were delighted to see that our birds, antelope, and rabbits were thriving in their new home. After several hours of exploring island, we decided that this was the ideal spot to erect a small fortification for protection in case of enemy attack. This required weeks of hard, back-breaking work, for we had to move our two cannons to the island and construct a wooden platform for them. It was a happy day when we gingerly set the cannons in place top of the platform and faced them toward toward the open sea. Then we raised the Swiss flag up the pole and watched it wave gaily in the breeze.

After our mission on Shark Island was completed, Fritz continued his explorations by cajack. On one occasion when his goal was to

Fritz Tests His Airtight Suit.

master the swift current of Jackal's River, he was thrown back into the ocean and nearly drowned. We discovered him hours afterward huddled on a large rock, all alone except for a walrus he had killed with a harpoon.

Later on, he cut off the walrus's head, stuffed it, and attached it to the bow of his cajack which, from that time on, he referred to as *The Walrus.*

Naming the Cajack *The Walrus*

"You Must Go In Search of Fritz."

CHAPTER 14

A Mysterious Message

Ten years had passed since our arrival in this part of the world. My sons were no longer boys, but grown men. Fritz was twenty-four years old; Jack was twenty-three; Ernest was twenty; and Francis was eighteen. It was almost impossible now to curtail their jaunts into unknown regions of the island.

One day Fritz left on an expedition that was to change all our lives. He set sail at daybreak and was gone the entire afternoon. Shortly before dusk, Elizabeth approached me frantically, "You must go in search of Fritz, my dear. I am so worried about him."

THE SWISS FAMILY ROBINSON

To relieve my wife's anxiety, my sons and I set out for Shark Island, where we fired the cannon as a signal to Fritz. A few minutes later we saw a black spot on the sea. Looking through my spyglass, I saw that it was my wandering son.

"Fritz, you gave us quite a fright!" I cried as he beached his cajack. "Thank heaven you are safe!"

"Oh, I'm fine, Father," said Fritz, unconcerned. "Wait till you see what I have. I think I've made a discovery that is worth more than all the treasures on earth."

"Tell us all about it," Ernest begged.

"Well," he began, "I was anxious to explore the eastern coast of the island, for none of us has ever been there before. As I sailed among the shoals and rocks covered with the nests of sea gulls, I saw sea lions, elephants, and walruses all playing in the water. Naturally, I was in a hurry to get out of their way and rowed as fast as I could. Suddenly, I came to

Fritz Has Made a Discovery.

a magnificent natural bridge which I passed under. The bridge led into a cave and out into a beautiful, calm bay. Peering down in the azure-blue water, I saw bed after bed of giant oysters.

"I caught some with a hook and tossed them over on the sand. However, when I opened them, instead of finding a nice fat oyster, there was only hard, gritty meat inside. Then, my knife hit some little, round hard stones the size of peas. I lifted them out and held them up to the light. "Pearls!' I cried in ectasy. 'Real pearls!' See, Father, I have brought back a whole box full."

"They really are pearls of rare quality!" I exclaimed, as we examined the contents of Fritz's box. "Son, you have discovered a valuable treasure."

"Something else happened on the trip," Fritz announced. "I found this linen note tied to the foot of a sea gull not far from the oyster beds."

Pearls of Rare Quality!

"Let me see it," I cried, opening up the message.

"What does it say?" asked Francis eagerly.

"It's written in English," I said, "and reads: 'Save the poor shipwrecked sailor on the smoking rock.'"

"How mysterious!" cried Jack. "Father, what do you think this means?"

"It means that we are no longer alone on this island. Somewhere, a lone sailor is waiting for us to rescue him."

A Message from a Shipwrecked Sailor

Fritz Has the Messenger.

CHAPTER 15

A Sailor Named Emily

We read and reread the message on the linen cloth to make sure it was real. Our one thought now was to search the coast for the "smoking rock" and to save the poor sailor stranded there.

"If only we had the bird who delivered this note to you, we could send an answer back," I remarked.

"Oh, I do have him, Father. He's tucked down in my sack," Fritz said, and he returned to his cajack to retrieve the sea gull.

While Fritz held the bird tightly in his arms, I wrote this short line: "Have faith in God.

Help is near." Then, I attached the slip to the sea gull's foot and threw the bird up in the air It flapped its wings and flew off toward the east.

"We mustn't forget the oyster beds, Father," Fritz reminded me, as I watched the bird disappear in the distance. "After all, itmay be some time before we get an answer to the note—if we get one at all."

The three of us spent the entire next day preparing our cargo. Then, with a soft breeze blowing we, too, embarked for the eastern coastline. Fritz and Jack led the way in the cajack, while Ernest and I steered the canoe loaded with equipment. At the last minute, young Knipps, the son of our first monkey, hopped in along with Turk and Flora.

At last, we reached our destination, which was as picturesque as Fritz had described it. As we sailed into the Bay of Pearls—for this is what we named it—we gasped, for the sight we saw took our breath away—we saw huge

Sailing into the Bay of Pearls

oyster beds nestled on the ocean floor.

We rested that night, and at dawn the next day we began our pearl fishery. With the aid of rakes, hooks, nets, and poles, we soon drew up large quantities of oysters. As they slowly popped open, we were delighted to see that each one contained a priceless, cream-colored pearl, shining brilliantly in the tropic sun.

That night, as we sat around our campfire discussing the exciting events of the day, we heard terrible noises coming from the jungle. We paid little attention to them until a short while later, when we heard the rustling bushes near our campsite. We looked up, and there, in the flickering light, stood an enormous lion, crouched down as if he was ready to spring. Just as I was preparing to fire, a shot rang out, and the animal lay dead.

"Bless you, Fritz!" I cried, "You have saved us from a horrible death!"

But Fritz never had time to reply. For the next second, a lioness, probably the mate of

A Priceless Pearl in Each Oyster

the dead lion, came leaping towards his body. She sniffed around the body and licked up his blood. Then she began to howl at the top of her lungs, as if announcing with those cries that she would devour us all.

Fritz fired again, and his bullet hit the lioness's shoulder. Now, the dogs rushed upon her and seized her flanks. I chose that opportunity to plunge my knife into her, but it was a costly victory. There, by the fire, slumped our beloved Flora, dead from the wounds the lioness had inflicted.

"Poor Flora!" wailed Jack. "She has done for us tonight what Grizzle did with the boa constrictor years ago."

I nodded and said solemnly to my sons, "We must give her a proper burial."

Flora received the honors of a torchlight funeral. We dug a grave and lowered our pet into it. Above the little mound we erected flat stone to mark her resting place. On it, we scratched her epitaph:

A Torchlight Funeral for Flora

Here lies
FLORA, A DOG
remarkable
for her courage and devotion.
She died under the claws of a lion
on whom she also inflicted death.

It was with heavy hearts that our canoe and cajack set sail for *Felsenheim* at sunrise. As we passed through the stone bridge, Fritz rowed up to our canoe and handed me a slip of paper. Then, to my surprise, he shot off like arrow. I quickly read his message: *"Dear Father, I am going alone in search of the sailor. Trust me and wish me luck. Fritz."*

Although I didn't like the idea of my son undertaking such a risky venture, there was no other course of action but to continue home.

Elizabeth was overjoyed with the luxurious lions' skins we brought back. Like me, she prayed that Fritz would be successful.

Five days passed and still there was no sign of our son. At Elizabeth's urging, the entire

Fritz Is Off To Find the Sailor.

family left on a searching trip around the east coast in our sailing ship. As we bobbed along on the sea, Ernest suddenly screamed out, "There's a man! A savage! Look at him!"

In the distance, we saw a strange man coming toward us in a canoe. Terror gripped me, for it appeared that we had indeed fallen upon a band of savages.

In one last desperate effort to avoid trouble, I called to the stranger in the Malay language, but he didn't answer. Then, I yelled out a few common sailing terms in English, and this time he waved a green branch over his head. Nearer and nearer he came, and finally we recognized the painted savage—it was none other than Fritz!

"What are you doing in that costume?" I called out as he drew up alongside us.

"I disguised myself because I was afraid I might run into an enemy. For a minute, I thought you were one. But let me tell you my good news. I have located the poor lost sailor."

A Savage Approaches in a Canoe.

THE SWISS FAMILY ROBINSON

"Who is he?" I asked. "What is his name?"

"The truth is, the sailor is really a girl and her name is Emily," Fritz whispered to me, cupping his hands around his mouth so his voice wouldn't carry.

"A girl! I don't believe you," I whispered back, although I don't know why I did so.

"It's absolutely true. And a very plucky girl she is too. For three years she has been living alone on the smoking rock. Now she is anxious to live with us, but she doesn't want anyone other than you and Mother to know she is a girl. Now come meet her."

We returned to shore to pick up Elizabeth, then followed Fritz. An hour later we arrived at a nearby island. After docking the ship, Fritz led us through some woods to a hut, where a low fire was burning.

"Hello," Fritz called out.

Down from a tree jumped a young and handsome sailor. "Hello," she said shyly. "I'm Sir Edward Montrose. "

A Young Sailor Jumps Down from a Tree.

Fritz Introduces the Sailor.

CHAPTER 16

A Sad Farewell

It had been such a long time since we had seen another human being that for several minutes we all stood spellbound, staring at the handsome young sailor.

Finally, Fritz broke the silence. Taking his new friend by the hand, he led her forward. "Mother, Father, please say hello," he urged.

"Hello," I said, recognizing immediately that the sailor was a girl.

"Welcome to our family," Elizabeth cried warmly.

This unexpected tenderness released Emily's pent-up emotions, and she rushed into

Elizabeth's arms in a flood of tears.

"How can I ever thank you for your kindness!" she wept.

As she spoke, my sons crowded near, and there were smiles and handshakes all around.

Over supper we all got acquainted. After a while the newcomer seemed tired, so Elizabeth escorted her down to the ship for the night.

For a long time afterward, we sat by the fire discussing this sudden turn of events. In the excitement of relating his adventure, Fritz forgot the secret he was supposed to keep, and the name Emily slipped out.

"Emily!" exclaimed Jack, shocked.

"Emily!" cried Francis. "Do you mean to tell us that Sir Edward is really a girl?"

"I'm afraid so," answered Fritz. "She pretended to be a boy because the sailor's suit is the only outfit she has worn in three years. She was too embarrassed to admit she was a girl until she had a dress to wear."

"Well, you'll have to give us time to get used

Tears of Happiness

to the idea that Emily is a girl," said Ernest.

The next morning when Emily arrived for breakfast, she had removed her sailor's cap, and her long blonde curls fell down on her shoulders. My sons were completely tongue-tied in the presence of such a beautiful English girl.

"I hope you don't mind my being a girl," Emily said shyly.

"Of course not," said Francis.

"I'm getting used to the idea already," quipped Ernest.

"Everyone is delighted," said Fritz. "Now we're just anxious for you to see *Felsenheim*. We hope you're going to like it there."

"I'm sure I will," Emily replied with a smile on her face.

Soon after, we set sail from Emily's island. When she took her first step on the sand at Providence Bay, her new brothers all shouted, "Hurrah! Welcome home! "

Fritz took her by the hand and led her up to

Emily Is a Beautiful English Girl.

the grotto. The rest of us followed behind.

"Oh, how beautiful," Emily murmured as she wandered through the rooms, admiring all we had done.

Elizabeth prepared an elegant dinner of roast turkey with truffles, wild rice, and fruit. A double spray of flowers hung over a sign which read, "Welcome, Emily Montrose."

As we lingered over dessert, Emily, who seemed more at ease with us now, told us more about herself. "I was born in India of English parents," she began, "but my mother died when I was three. I was raised by my father, an officer in the British Navy.

"When he and his regiment were ordered back to England, we sailed on separate ships. It's a rule that women cannot ride on a battleship in time of war. So I boarded a ship whose captain was a good friend of my father. After a few days we ran into a storm and were shipwrecked.

"Like you, I made my way to this island, but

Emily Tells About Herself.

THE SWISS FAMILY ROBINSON

I lay on the beach for a long time near death. When I awoke, I ate shellfish to regain my strength. My training in sports enabled me to build a sturdy hut with a framework of stout poles and bamboo, walls woven with reeds, and a thatched roof of palm leaves and clay.

"I tamed and trained a cormorant to spear fish, strike down birds, and catch geese, rabbits, and other small animals. So I have never gone hungry or lacked for companionship. At all times I kept a fire burning at the end of the reef, hoping to attract a passing ship. Now I am lucky enough to be living in your lovely home."

"We think we're the lucky ones," Elizabeth said, "for we have a new daughter."

"And we have an adopted sister," cried Francis. "Now our life is really complete."

Our life went on pleasantly for some time until one day when something happened to change this peaceful existence. On a trip to Shark Island, Jack and Fritz mischievously

Emily Built a Sturdy Hut.

set off several cannon blasts. To their surprise, they heard an answer in the distance. Wide eyed, they returned to inform me of this strange happening.

"If there is really a ship on our coast, we don't know whether it is manned by Europeans or by Malay pirates," I said. "I don't know whether to be happy or sad."

We all rushed down to the beach, and there, on the coast, we spotted a fine European ship sailing toward us. An English flag floated from the masthead.

To be on the safe side, we hid in the bushes as the ship dropped anchor and the sailors rowed to shore. They set up tents and roasted meat for dinner. After a while two sentinels spied us, and we came out of hiding.

"Welcome, Englishmen!" we cried. But they kept their distance, and we kept ours.

Later, we sailed out to the ship, the *Unicorn*, and gave the captain a warm welcome. He was relieved to see we were not savages, and he

An English Ship Arrives.

conducted us to his cabin where a glass of wine sealed our friendship.

Good fortune was smiling on us, for the captain, Captain Littleton, was a friend of Commander Montrose, and he eagerly assured Emily that her father was alive.

"I also have an Englishman on board I want you to meet," he said. "A Mr. Wolston, his wife, and two daughters."

Elizabeth was overjoyed to have company, and she prepared a gala dinner, after which she insisted that the Wolstons stay at *Felsenheim*.

The next morning, Mr. Wolston approached me and said, "My wife and I are so impressed by your life here that we wonder if we could live on the island too?"

"Of course, my good man," I said, slapping him on the back. "It will be wonderful to have neighbors at long last."

Despite my delight at the Wolston's decision to become citizens of our island, I began to wonder just how wise it would be for my

A Glass of Wine with the Captain

children to live here forever. Although Elizabeth and I had no desire to return to Europe, I thought our sons should at least be offered the opportunity.

I gathered my family together and discussed the matter with them frankly. Ernest and Jack immediately stated that they were content here, but Fritz fell silent. After a bit, he confessed that he and Francis would like to sail back to Europe together.

For eight days, the *Unicorn* remained at anchor while we packed a valuable cargo of pearls, spices, furs, and ivory for our sons to sell in Europe.

And then came the day when the ship was to sail. A cannon blast announced the hour of departure. After many handshakes and tender hugs, Fritz and Francis climbed aboard. They stood on the deck waving good-bye.

"Have a good trip!" we cried as the *Unicorn* slowly slipped away.

We watched until the ship was merely a

Tender Hugs

black speck on the horizon.

"Good-bye, my sons," Elizabeth and I whispered, brushing the tears away.

It was a sad moment, for we knew in our hearts that we had said our last farewell to Europe and our beloved Switzerland.

A Last Farewell